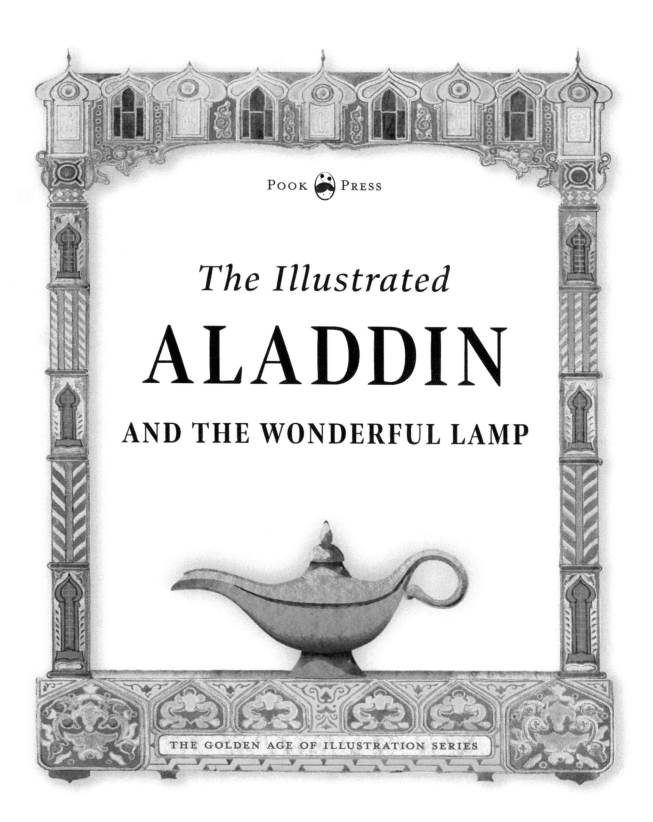

POOK ● PRESS

The Illustrated
ALADDIN
AND THE WONDERFUL LAMP

THE GOLDEN AGE OF ILLUSTRATION SERIES

POOK PRESS

Copyright © 2019 Pook Press
An imprint of Read Publishing Ltd.

Home Farm, 44 Evesham Road, Cookhill, Alcester,
Warwickshire, B49 5LJ

Design by Zoë Horn Haywood
Edited by S. Bigland

British Library Cataloguing-in-Publication Data.
A catalogue record for this book is available from
the British Library.

www.pookpress.co.uk

CONTENTS

Where captions have been sourced from the original books, the text may differ due to varying translations of *Aladdin and the Wonderful Lamp*.

You can find a list of all the source books in the bibliography at the back of this book.

LIST OF FULL PAGE ILLUSTRATIONS

The Slave of the Lamp.
Illustrated by Thomas Mackenzie

Introduction

to

THE GOLDEN AGE OF ILLUSTRATION

The 'Golden age of Illustration' refers to a period customarily defined as lasting from the latter quarter of the nineteenth century until just after the First World War. In this period of no more than fifty years the popularity, abundance and most importantly the unprecedented upsurge in quality of illustrated works marked an astounding change in the way that publishers, artists and the general public came to view this hitherto insufficiently esteemed art form.

Until the latter part of the nineteenth century, the work of illustrators was largely proffered anonymously, and in England it was only after Thomas Bewick's pioneering technical advances in wood engraving that it became common to acknowledge the artistic and technical expertise of book and magazine illustrators. Although widely regarded as the patriarch of the *Golden Age*, Walter Crane (1845-1915) started his career as an anonymous illustrator – gradually building his reputation through striking designs, famous for their sharp outlines and flat tints of colour. Like many other great illustrators to follow, Crane operated within many different mediums; a lifelong disciple of William Morris and a member of the Arts and Crafts Movement, he designed all manner of objects including wallpaper, furniture, ceramic ware and even whole interiors. This incredibly important and inclusive phase of British design proved to have a lasting impact on illustration both in the United Kingdom and Europe as well as America.

The artists involved in the Arts and Crafts Movement attempted to counter the ever intruding Industrial Revolution (the first wave of which lasted roughly from 1750-1850) by bringing the values of beautiful and inventive craftsmanship back into the sphere of everyday life. It must be noted that around the turn of the century the boundaries between what would today be termed 'fine art' as opposed to 'crafts' and 'design' were far more fluid and in many cases non-operational, and many illustrators had lucrative painterly careers in addition to their design work. The Romanticism of the *Pre Raphaelite Brotherhood* combined with the intricate curvatures of the *Art Nouveaux* movement provided influential strands running through most illustrators work. The latter especially so for the Scottish illustrator Anne Anderson (1874-1930) as well as the Dutch artist Kay Nielson (1886-1957), who was also inspired by the stunning work of Japanese artists such as Hiroshige.

One of the main accomplishments of nineteenth century illustration lay in its ability to reach far wider numbers than the traditional 'high arts'. In 1892 the American critic William A. Coffin praised the new medium for popularising art; 'more has been done through the medium of illustrated literature… to make the masses of people realise that there is such a thing as art and that it is worth caring about'. Commercially, illustrated publications reached their zenith with the burgeoning 'Gift Book' industry which emerged in the first decade of the twentieth century. The first widely distributed gift book was published in 1905. It comprised of Washington Irving's short story *Rip Van Winkle* with the addition of 51 colour plates by a true master of illustration; Arthur Rackham. Rackham created each plate by first painstakingly drawing his subject in a sinuous pencil line before applying an ink layer – then he used layer upon layer of delicate watercolours to build up the romantic yet calmly ethereal results on which his reputation was constructed. Although Rackham is now one of the most recognisable names in illustration, his delicate palette owed no small debt to Kate Greenaway (1846-1901) – one of the first female illustrators whose pioneering and incredibly subtle use of the watercolour medium resulted in her election to the Royal Institute of Painters in Water Colours in 1889.

The year before Arthur Rackam's illustrations for *Rip Van Winkle* were published, a young and aspiring French artist by the name of Edmund Dulac (1882-1953) came to London and was to create a similarly impressive legacy. His timing could not have been more fortuitous. Several factors converged around the turn of the century which allowed illustrators and publishers alike a far greater freedom of creativity than previously imagined. The origination of the 'colour separation' practice meant that colour images, extremely faithful to the original artwork could be produced on a grand scale. Dulac possessed a rigorously painterly background (more so than his contemporaries) and was hence able to utilise the new technology so as to allow the colour itself to refine and define an object as opposed to the traditional pen and ink line. It has been estimated that in 1876 there was only one 'colour separation' firm in London, but by 1900 this number had rocketed to fifty. This improvement in printing quality also meant a reduction in labour, and coupled with the introduction of new presses and low-cost supplies of paper this meant that publishers could for the first time afford to pay high wages for highly talented artists.

Whilst still in the U.K. no survey of the *Golden Age of Illustration* would be complete without a mention of the Heath-Robinson brothers. Charles Robinson was renowned for his beautifully detached style, whether in pen and ink or sumptuous watercolours. Whilst William (the youngest) was to later garner immense fame for his carefully constructed yet tortuous machines operated by comical, intensely serious attendants. After World War One the Robinson brothers numbered among the few artists of the Golden Age who continued to regularly produce illustrated works. As we move towards the United States, one illustrator - Howard Pyle (1853-1911) stood head and shoulders above his contemporaries as the most distinguished illustrator of the age. From 1880 onwards Pyle illustrated over 100 volumes, yet it was not quantity which ensured his precedence over other American (and European) illustrators, but quality.

Pyle's sumptuous illustrations benefitted from a meticulous composition process livened with rich colour and deep recesses, providing a visual framework in which tales such as *Robin Hood* and *The Four Volumes of the Arthurian Cycle* could come to life. These are publications which remain continuous good sellers up till the present day. His flair and originality combined with a thoroughness of planning and execution were principles which he passed onto his many pupils at the *Drexel Institute of Arts and Sciences*. Two such pupils were Jessie Willcox Smith (1863-1935) who went on to illustrate books such as *The Water Babies* and *At the Back of the North Wind* and perhaps most famously Maxfield Parrish (1870-1966) who became famed for luxurious colour (most remarkably demonstrated in his blue paintings) and imaginative designs; practices in no short measure gleaned from his tutor. As an indication of Parrish's popularity, in 1925 it was estimated that one fifth of American households possessed a Parrish reproduction.

As is evident from this brief introduction to the 'Golden Age of Illustration', it was a period of massive technological change and artistic ingenuity. The legacy of this enormously important epoch lives on in the present day – in the continuing popularity and respect afforded to illustrators, graphic and fine artists alike. The present volume provides a fascinating insight into an era of intense historical and creative development, bringing out of print books and their art back to life for both young and old to revel and delight in.

We hope that the current reader adores this book as much as we do. Enjoy.

Amelia Carruthers

Aladdin finds the lamp.
Illustrated by Walter Crane

The Illustrated
Aladdin and the Wonderful Lamp

He generally went out early in the morning, and spent the whole day playing in the public streets with other boys about the same age, who were as idle as himself.
Illustrated by Felix O. C. Darley

Illustrator: John Hassall

There once lived a poor tailor, who had a son called Aladdin, a careless, idle boy who would do nothing but play ball all day long in the streets with little idle boys like himself. This so grieved the father that he died; yet, in spite of his mother's tears and prayers, Aladdin did not mend his ways. One day, when he was playing in the streets as usual, a stranger asked him his age, and if he was not the son of Mustapha the tailor. "I am, sir," replied Aladdin; "but he died a long while ago."

The African magician embracing Aladdin.
Engraved by the Brothers Dalziel

Illustrator: Louis Rhead

On this the stranger, who was a famous African magician, fell on his neck and kissed him, saying, "I am your uncle, and knew you from your likeness to my brother. Go to your mother and tell her I am coming." Aladdin ran home and told his mother of his newly found uncle. "Indeed, child," she said, "your father had a brother, but I always thought he was dead." However, she prepared supper, and bade Aladdin seek his uncle, who came laden with wine and fruit. He presently fell down and kissed the place where Mustapha used to sit, bidding Aladdin's mother not to be surprised at not having seen him before, as he had been forty years out of the country.

A stranger asked him his age, and if he was not the son of Mustapha the tailor.
Illustrated by Felix O. C. Darley

Illustrator: Walter Paget

He then turned to Aladdin, and asked him his trade, at which the boy hung his head, while his mother burst into tears. On learning that Aladdin was idle and would learn no trade, he offered to take a shop for him and stock it with merchandise.

Next day he bought Aladdin a fine suit of clothes and took him all over the city, showing him the sights, and brought him home at nightfall to his mother, who was overjoyed to see her son so fine.

Next day he bought Aladdin a fine suit of clothes.
Illustrated by John Hassall

There he entered a clothier's shop containing all kinds of clothes.
Illustrated by René Bull

So they took a seat over against a lakelet and rested a little while.

Illustrated by René Bull

Illustrator: Walter Paget

The next day the magician led Aladdin into some beautiful gardens a long way outside the city gates. They sat down by a fountain and the magician pulled a cake from his girdle, which he divided between them. They then journeyed onward till they almost reached the mountains. Aladdin was so tired that he begged to go back, but the magician beguiled him with pleasant stories, and led him on in spite of himself. At last they came to two mountains divided by a narrow valley. "We will go no farther," said the false uncle.

Illustrator: Sidney H. Heath (Above)

Aladdin and the magician.
Illustrated by Thomas Mackenzie (Right)

12

"I will show you something wonderful; only do you gather up sticks while I kindle a fire." When it was lit the magician threw on it a powder he had about him, at the same time saying some magical words. The earth trembled a little and opened in front of them, disclosing a square flat stone with a brass ring in the middle to raise it by. Aladdin tried to run away, but the magician caught him and gave him a blow that knocked him down. "What have I done, uncle?" he said piteously; whereupon the magician said more kindly: "Fear nothing, but obey me."

Illustrator: Charles Robinson

The magician threw on it a powder he had about him.
Illustrated by Felix O. C. Darley

Illustrator: Robert Pimlott

"Beneath this stone lies a treasure which is to be yours, and no one else may touch it, so you must do exactly as I tell you." At the word treasure Aladdin forgot his fears, and grasped the ring as he was told, saying the names of his father and grandfather. The stone came up quite easily, and some steps appeared. "Go down," said the magician; "at the foot of those steps you will find an open door leading into three large halls. Tuck up your gown and go through them without touching anything, or you will die instantly. These halls lead into a garden of fine fruit trees. Walk on until you come to a niche in a terrace where stands a lighted lamp. Pour out the oil it contains, and bring it to me." He drew a ring from his finger and gave it to Aladdin, bidding him prosper.

The earth trembled.
Illustrated by H. G. Theaker

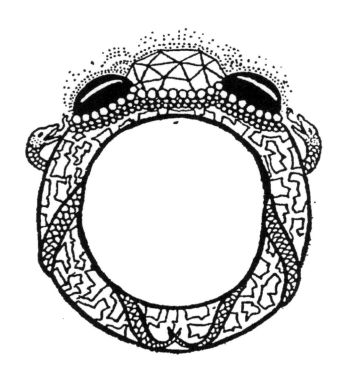

Illustrator: Thomas Mackenzie (Above)

The Garden of the Lamp.
Illustrated by John Hassall (Right)

The Magic Lamp.
Illustrated by Felix O. C. Darley

Illustrator: Thomas Mackenzie

Aladdin found everything as the magician had said, gathered some fruit off the trees, and, having got the lamp, arrived at the mouth of the cave. The magician cried out in a great hurry: "Make haste and give me the lamp." This Aladdin refused to do until he was out of the cave. The magician flew into a terrible passion, and throwing some more powder on to the fire, he said something, and the stone rolled back into its place.

"Make haste and give me the lamp."
Engraved by the Brothers Dalziel

Aladdin finds the Magic Lamp.
Illustrated by Edmund Dulac

The magician persisted in demanding the lamp before
he helped Aladdin out of the cave.
Illustrated by Louis Rhead

Illustrator: Thomas Mackenzie

The magician left Persia for ever, which plainly showed that he was no uncle of Aladdin's, but a cunning magician, who had read in his magic books of a wonderful lamp, which would make him the most powerful man in the world. Though he alone knew where to find it, he could only receive it from the hand of another. He had picked out the foolish Aladdin for this purpose, intending to get the lamp and kill him afterward.

Illustrator: Sidney H. Heath

For two days Aladdin remained in the dark, crying and lamenting. At last he clasped his hands in prayer, and in so doing rubbed the ring, which the magician had forgotten to take from him.

Immediately an enormous and frightful genie rose out of the earth, saying: "What wouldst thou with me? I am the Slave of the Ring, and will obey thee in all things." Aladdin fearlessly replied: "Deliver me from this place!" whereupon the earth opened, and he found. himself outside. As soon as his eyes could bear the light he went home, but fainted on the threshold.

For two days Aladdin remained in the dark.
Illustrated by Thomas Mackenzie

For two days Aladdin remained in the dark.
Illustrated by Felix O. C. Darley

Immediately a genie of enormous size rose out of the earth.
Illustrated by Monro S. Orr

Illustrator: H. G. Theaker (Above)

*One of the Jann whose favour was frightful
and whose bulk was horrible big.*
Illustrated by René Bull (Right)

A genie of enormous size rose out of the earth.
Illustrated by Walter Paget

When he came to himself he told his mother what had passed, and showed her the lamp and the fruits he had gathered in the garden, which were, in reality, precious stones. He then asked for some food. "Alas! child," she said, "I have nothing in the house, but I have spun a little cotton and will go and sell it." Aladdin bade her keep her cotton, for he would sell the lamp instead. As it was very dirty she began to rub it, that it might fetch a higher price. Instantly a hideous genie appeared, and asked what she would have. She fainted away, but Aladdin, snatching the lamp, said boldly: "Fetch me something to eat!" The genie returned with a silver bowl, twelve silver plates containing rich meats, two silver cups, and two bottles of wine. Aladdin's mother, when she came to herself, said: "Whence comes this splendid feast?" "Ask not, but eat," replied Aladdin.

Illustrator: John Hassall

So they sat at breakfast till it was dinner-time, and Aladdin told his mother about the lamp. She begged him to sell it, and have nothing to do with devils. "No," said Aladdin, "since chance hath made us aware of its virtues, we will use it, and the ring likewise, which I shall always wear on my finger." When they had eaten all the genie had brought, Aladdin sold one of the silver plates, and so on until none were left. He then had recourse to the genie, who gave him another set of plates, and thus they lived for many years.

Illustrator: Charles Robinson

The slave to the ring appears to Aladdin.
Illustrated by H. J. Ford

Illustrator: Thomas Mackenzie (Above)

Aladdin finds the Efrite.
Illustrated by Edmund Dulac (Right)

Aladdin commanded the Slave of the Lamp to bring him something to eat.
Illustrated by Arthur Rackham

The genie immediately returned with a tray bearing dishes of the most delicious viands.
Illustrated by Milo Winter

One day Aladdin heard an order from the Sultan proclaimed that everyone was to stay at home and close his shutters while the Princess, his daughter, went to and from the bath. Aladdin was seized by a desire to see her face, which was very difficult, as she always went veiled. He hid himself behind the door of the bath, and peeped through a chink. The Princess lifted her veil as she went in, and looked so beautiful that Aladdin fell in love with her at first sight. He went home so changed that his mother was frightened. He told her he loved the Princess so deeply that he could not live without her, and meant to ask her in marriage of her father. His mother, on hearing this, burst out laughing, but Aladdin at last prevailed upon her to go before the Sultan and carry his request.

Illustrator: Sidney H. Heath

The Sultan proclaimed that everyone was to stay at home and close his shutters.
Illustrated by Sidney H. Heath

The Princess, his daughter, went to and from the bath.
Illustrated by Felix O. C. Darley

The Lady Bedr-el-Budur at her bath.
Illustrated by Edmund Dulac

The Princess lifted her veil as she went in.
Engraved by the Brothers Dalziel

When she had come within three or four paces of
the door of the bath she lifted up the veil.
Illustrated by Louis Rhead

Illustrator: Thomas Mackenzie (Above)

The Princess lifted her veil.
Illustrated by Walter Crane (Right)

She fetched a napkin and laid in it the magic fruits from the enchanted garden, which sparkled and shone like the most beautiful jewels. She took these with her to please the Sultan, and set out, trusting in the lamp. The Grand Vizier and the lords of council had just gone in as she entered the hall and placed herself in front of the Sultan. He, however, took no notice of her. She went every day for a week, and stood in the same place. When the council broke up on the sixth day the Sultan said to his Vizier: "I see a certain woman in the audience-chamber every day carrying something in a napkin. Call her next time, that I may find out what she wants." Next day, at a sign from the Vizier, she went up to the foot of the throne and remained kneeling till the Sultan said to her: "Rise, good woman, and tell me what you want." She hesitated, so the Sultan sent away all but the Vizier, and bade her speak frankly, promising to forgive

Engraved by the Brothers Dalziel

Illustrator: Robert Pimlott

her beforehand for anything she might say. She then told him of her son's violent love for the Princess. "I prayed him to forget her," she said, "but in vain; he threatened to do some desperate deed if I refused to go and ask your Majesty for the hand of the Princess. Now I pray you to forgive not me alone, but my son Aladdin." The Sultan asked her kindly what she had in the napkin, whereupon she unfolded the jewels and presented them. He was thunderstruck, and turning to the Vizier said: "What sayest thou? Ought I not to bestow the Princess on one who values her at such a price?" The Vizier, who wanted her for his own son, begged the Sultan to withhold her for three months, in the course of which he hoped his son would contrive to make him a richer present. The Sultan granted this, and told Aladdin's mother that, though he consented to the marriage, she must not appear before him again for three months.

She unfolded the jewels and presented them.
Engraved by the Brothers Dalziel.

She went every day for a week.
Illustrated by Sidney H. Heath

Illustrator: Thomas Mackenzie

Aladdin waited patiently for nearly three months, but after two had elapsed his mother, going into the city to buy oil, found every one rejoicing, and asked what was going on. "Do you not know," was the answer, "that the son of the Grand Vizier is to marry the Sultan's daughter to-night?" Breathless, she ran and told Aladdin, who was overwhelmed at first, but presently bethought him of the lamp. He rubbed it, and the genie appeared, saying, "What is thy will?" Aladdin replied: "The Sultan, as thou knowest, has broken his promise to me, and the Vizier's son is to have the Princess. My command is that to-night you bring hither the bride and bridegroom." "Master, I obey," said the genie. Aladdin then went to his chamber, where, sure enough, at midnight the genie transported the bed containing the Vizier's son and the Princess. "Take this new-married man," he said, "and put him outside in the cold, and return at daybreak." Whereupon the genie took the Vizier's son out of bed, leaving Aladdin with the Princess. "Fear nothing," Aladdin said to her; "you are my wife, promised to me by your unjust father, and no harm shall come to you." The Princess was too frightened to speak, and passed the most miserable night of her life, while Aladdin lay down beside her and slept soundly. At the appointed hour the genie fetched in the shivering bridegroom, laid him in his place, and transported the bed back to the palace.

Illustrator: Unknown

Put him outside in the cold.
Engraved by the Brothers Dalziel.

Presently the Sultan came to wish his daughter good-morning. The unhappy Vizier's son jumped up and hid himself, while the Princess would not say a word, and was very sorrowful. The Sultan sent her mother to her, who said: "How comes it, child, that you will not speak to your father? What has happened?" The Princess sighed deeply, and at last told her mother how, during the night, the bed had been carried into some strange house, and what had passed there. Her mother did not believe her in the least, but bade her rise and consider it an idle dream.

Illustrator: H. G. Theaker

The following night exactly the same thing happened, and next morning, on the Princess's refusal to speak, the Sultan threatened to cut off her head. She then confessed all, bidding him to ask the Vizier's son if it were not so. The Sultan told the Vizier to ask his son, who owned the truth, adding that, dearly as he loved the Princess, he had rather die than go through another such fearful night, and wished to be separated from her. His wish was granted, and there was an end to feasting and rejoicing.

When the three months were over, Aladdin sent his mother to remind the Sultan of his promise. She stood in the same place as before, and the Sultan, who had forgotten Aladdin, at once remembered him, and sent for her. On seeing her poverty the Sultan felt less inclined than ever to keep his word, and asked his Vizier's advice, who counselled him to set so high a value on the Princess that no man living could come up to it. The Sultan then turned to Aladdin's mother, saying: "Good woman, a Sultan must remember his promises, and I will remember mine, but your son must first send me forty basins of gold brimful of jewels, carried by forty black slaves, led by as many white ones, splendidly dressed. Tell him that I await his answer."

Illustrator: Sidney H. Heath

Forty basins of gold brimful of jewels.
Illustrated by Thomas Mackenzie

Illustrator: Sidney H. Heath (Above)

The house was filled with slaves bearing basons of massy gold.
Illustrated by Charles Robinson (Right)

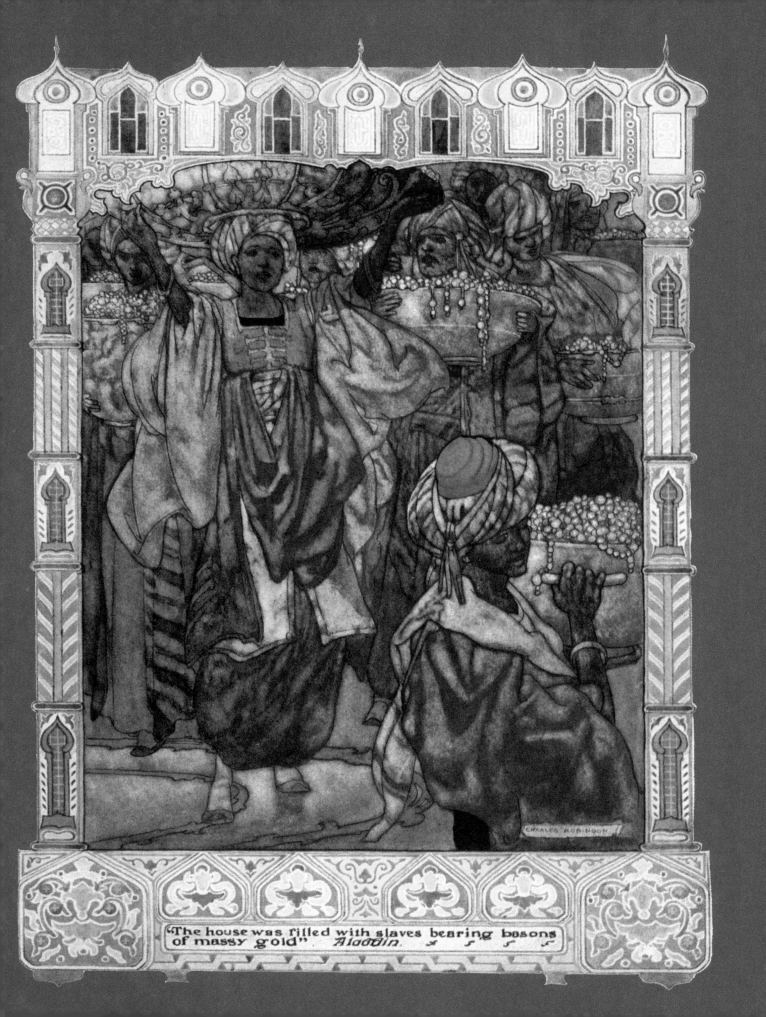

"The house was filled with slaves bearing basons of massy gold" *Aladdin.*

Aladdin's mother brings the slaves with the forty basins of gold before the Sultan.
Illustrated by H. J. Ford

*They were so richly dressed, with such splendid jewels in their girdles,
that everyone crowded to see them.*
Illustrated by Walter Crane

The mother of Aladdin bowed low and went home, thinking all was lost. She gave Aladdin the message, adding: "He may wait long enough for your answer!" "Not so long, mother, as you think," her son replied. "I would do a great deal more than that for the Princess." He summoned the genie, and in a few moments the eighty slaves arrived, and filled up the small house and garden. Aladdin made them set out to the palace, two and two, followed by his mother. They were so richly dressed, with such splendid jewels in their girdles, that everyone crowded to see them and the basins of gold they carried on their heads. They entered the palace, and, after kneeling before the Sultan, stood in a half-circle round the throne with their arms crossed, while Aladdin's mother presented them to the Sultan. He hesitated no longer, but said: "Good woman, return and tell your son that I wait for him with open arms."

Illustrator: Thomas Mackenzie

The Lady Bedr-el-Budur.
Illustrated by Edmund Dulac

Illustrator: Robert Pimlott (Above)

Kneeling before the Sultan.
Illustrated by Thomas Mackenzie (Right)

*By the aid of the Fairy he attired himself in a dress
much richer than was ever worn by a King.*
Illustrated by A. Guthrie

She lost no time in telling Aladdin, bidding him make haste. But Aladdin first called the genie. "I want a scented bath," he said, "a richly embroidered habit, a horse surpassing the Sultan's, and twenty slaves to attend me. Besides this, six slaves, beautifully dressed, to wait on my mother; and lastly, ten thousand pieces of gold in ten purses." No sooner said than done. Aladdin mounted his horse and passed through the streets, the slaves strewing gold as they went. Those who had played with him in his childhood knew him not, he had grown so handsome. When the Sultan saw him he came down from his throne, embraced him, and led him into a hall where a feast was spread, intending to marry him to the Princess that very day. But Aladdin refused, saying, "I must build a palace fit for her," and took his leave. Once home, he said to the genie: "Build me a palace of the finest marble, set with jasper, agate, and other precious stones. In the middle you shall build me a large hall with a dome, its four walls of massy gold and silver, each having six windows, whose lattices, all except one which is to be left unfinished, must be set with diamonds and rubies. There must be stables and horses and grooms and slaves; go and see about it!"

Illustrator: Thomas Mackenzie

Aladdin rides to the Sultan's palace.
Illustrated by Charles Robinson

Illustrator: John Hassall

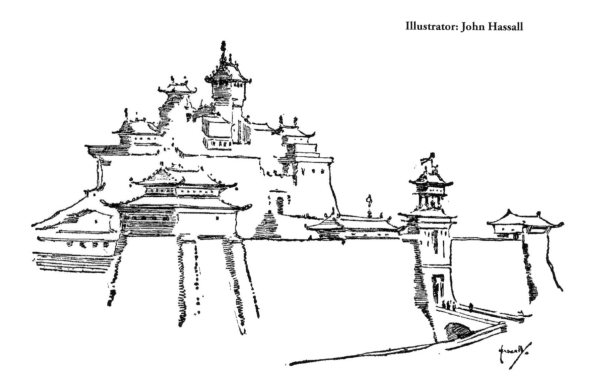

The palace was finished by the next day, and the genie carried him there and showed him all his orders faithfully carried out, even to the laying of a velvet carpet from Aladdin's palace to the Sultan's. Aladdin's mother then dressed herself carefully, and walked to the palace with her slaves, while he followed her on horseback. The Sultan sent musicians with trumpets and cymbals to meet them, so that the air resounded with music and cheers. She was taken to the Princess, who saluted her and treated her with great honor. At night the Princess said good-by to her father, and set out on the carpet for Aladdin's palace, with his mother at her side, and followed by the hundred slaves. She was charmed at the sight of Aladdin, who ran to receive her. "Princess," he said, "blame your beauty for my boldness if I have displeased you."

She told him that, having seen him, she willingly obeyed her father in this matter. After the wedding had taken place Aladdin led her into the hall, where a feast was spread, and she supped with him, after which they danced till midnight. Next day Aladdin invited the Sultan to see the palace. On entering the hall with the four-and-twenty windows, with their rubies, diamonds, and emeralds, he cried: "It is a world's wonder! There is only one thing that surprises me. Was it by accident that one window was left unfinished?" "No, sir, by design," returned Aladdin. "I wished your Majesty to have the glory of finishing this palace." The Sultan was pleased, and sent for the best jewelers in the city. He showed them the unfinished window, and bade them fit it up like the others.

Illustrator: H. G. Theaker

The Nuptial Dance of Aladdin and the Lady Bedr-el-Budur.
Illustrated by Edmund Dulac

Illustrator: Sidney H. Heath

"Sir," replied their spokesman, "we cannot find jewels enough." The Sultan had his own fetched, which they soon used, but to no purpose, for in a month's time the work was not half done. Aladdin, knowing that their task was vain, bade them undo their work and carry the jewels back, and the genie finished the window at his command. The Sultan was surprised to receive his jewels again, and visited Aladdin, who showed him the window finished. The Sultan embraced him, the envious Vizier meanwhile hinting that it was the work of enchantment.

Aladdin invited the Sultan to see the palace.
Illustrated by Thomas Mackenzie

Illustrator: Thomas Mackenzie

Aladdin had won the hearts of the people by his gentle bearing. He was made captain of the Sultan's armies, and won several battles for him, but remained modest and courteous as before, and lived thus in peace and content for several years.

But far away in Africa the magician remembered Aladdin, and by his magic arts discovered that Aladdin, instead of perishing miserably in the cave, had escaped, and had married a princess, with whom he was living in great honor and wealth. He knew that the poor tailor's son could only have accomplished this by means of the lamp, and traveled night and day until he reached the capital of China, bent on Aladdin's ruin. As he passed through the town he heard people talking everywhere about a marvellous palace. "Forgive my ignorance," he asked, "what is this palace you speak Of?" "Have you not heard of Prince Aladdin's palace," was the reply, "the greatest wonder of the world? I will direct you if you have a mind to see it." The magician thanked him who spoke, and having seen the palace, knew that it had been raised by the Genie of the Lamp, and became half mad with rage. He determined to get hold of the lamp, and again plunge Aladdin into the deepest poverty.

Illustrator: Thomas Mackenzie

New lamps for old.
Illustrated by Walter Crane

Unluckily, Aladdin had gone a-hunting for eight days, which gave the magician plenty of time. He bought a dozen copper lamps, put them into a basket, and went to the palace, crying: "New lamps for old!" followed by a jeering crowd. The Princess, sitting in the hall of four-and-twenty windows, sent a slave to find out what the noise was about, who came back laughing, so that the Princess scolded her. "Madam," replied the slave, "who can help laughing to see an old fool offering to exchange fine new lamps for old ones?" Another slave, hearing this, said: "There is an old one on the cornice there which he can have." Now this was the magic lamp, which Aladdin had left there, as he could not take it out hunting with him. The Princess, not knowing its value, laughingly bade the slave take it and make the exchange.

Illustrator: John Hassall

Illustrator: H. G. Theaker

She went and said to the magician: "Give me a new lamp for this." He snatched it and bade the slave take her choice, amid the jeers of the crowd. Little he cared, but left off crying his lamps, and went out of the city gates to a lonely place, where he remained till nightfall, when he pulled out the lamp and rubbed it. The genie appeared, and at the magician's command carried him, together with the palace and the Princess in it, to a lonely place in Africa.

"Who will change old lamps for new ones?"
Illustrated by Monro S. Orr

The African magician gets the lamp from the slave.
Illustrated by H. J. Ford

New lamps for old.
Illustrated by Thomas Mackenzie

Illustrator: John Hassall (Above)

New lamps for old.
Illustrated by Arthur Rackham (Right)

"Who will exchange old lamps for new ones?"
Illustrated by Louis Rhead

"Give me a new lamp for this."
Illustrated by Felix O. C. Darley

Next morning the Sultan looked out of the window toward Aladdin's palace and rubbed his eyes, for it was gone. He sent for the Vizier and asked what had become of the palace. The Vizier looked out too, and was lost in astonishment. He again put it down to enchantment, and this time the Sultan believed him, and sent thirty men on horseback to fetch Aladdin in chains. They met him riding home, bound him, and forced him to go with them on foot.

Engraved by the Brothers Dalziel

The Sultan and his Vizier looking for Aladdin's magic palace.
Illustrated by Edmund Dulac

The people, however, who loved him, followed, armed, to see that he came to no harm. He was carried before the Sultan, who ordered the executioner to cut off his head. The executioner made Aladdin kneel down, bandaged his eyes, and raised his scimitar to strike. At that instant the Vizier, who saw that the crowd had forced their way into the courtyard and were scaling the walls to rescue Aladdin, called to the executioner to stay his hand. The people, indeed, looked so threatening that the Sultan gave way and ordered Aladdin to be unbound, and pardoned him in the sight of the crowd. Aladdin now begged to know what he had done. "False wretch!" said the Sultan, "come thither," and showed him from the window the place where his palace had stood. Aladdin was so amazed that he could not say a word. "Where is my palace and my daughter?" demanded the Sultan. "For the first I am not so deeply concerned, but my daughter I must have, and you must find her or lose your head."

**Illustrator:
Charles Robinson**

Illustrator: Robert Pimlott

Aladdin begged for forty days in which to find her, promising, if he failed, to return and suffer death at the Sultan's pleasure. His prayer was granted, and he went forth sadly from the Sultan's presence. For three days he wandered about like a madman, asking everyone what had become of his palace, but they only laughed and pitied him. He came to the banks of a river, and knelt down to say his prayers before throwing himself in. In so doing he rubbed the magic ring he still wore. The genie he had seen in the cave appeared, and asked his will. "Save my life, genie," said Aladdin, "bring my palace back." "That is not in my power," said the genie; "I am only the Slave of the Ring; you must ask him of the lamp." "Even so," said Aladdin, "but thou canst take me to the palace, and set me down under my dear wife's window." He at once found himself in Africa, under the window of the Princess, and fell asleep out of sheer weariness.

He came to the banks of a river.
Engraved by the Brothers Dalziel

He saw plainly that all his misfortunes were owing to the loss of the lamp,
and vainly wondered who had robbed him of it.
Illustrated by Thomas Mackenzie

Illustrator: John Hassall

He was awakened by the singing of the birds, and his heart was lighter. He saw plainly that all his misfortunes were owing to the loss of the lamp, and vainly wondered who had robbed him of it.

That morning the Princess rose earlier than she had done since she had been carried into Africa by the magician, whose company she was forced to endure once a day. She, however, treated him so harshly that he dared not live there altogether. As she was dressing, one of her women looked out and saw Aladdin. The Princess ran and opened the window, and at the noise she made Aladdin looked up.

Aladdin saluted her with an air that expresses his joy.
Illustrated by Walter Paget

She called to him to come to her, and great was the joy of these lovers at seeing each other again. After he had kissed her Aladdin said: "I beg of you, Princess, in God's name, before we speak of anything else, for your own sake and mine, tell me that has become of an old lamp I left on the cornice in the hall of four-and-twenty windows, when I went a-hunting." "Alas!" she said, "I am the innocent cause of our sorrows," and told him of the exchange of the lamp. "Now I know," cried Aladdin, "that we have to thank the African magician for this! Where is the lamp?" "He carries it about with him," said the Princess. "I know, for he pulled it out of his breast to show me.

Illustrator: Sidney H. Heath

Aladdin finds the Princess in Africa.
Illustrated by Edmund Dulac

Illustrator: H. G. Theaker

He wishes me to break my faith with you and marry him, saying that you were beheaded by my father's command. He is for ever speaking ill of you but I only reply by my tears. If I persist, I doubt not but he will use violence." Aladdin comforted her, and left her for a while. He changed clothes with the first person he met in the town, and having bought a certain powder, returned to the Princess, who let him in by a little side door. "Put on your most beautiful dress," he said to her "and receive the magician with smiles, leading him to believe that you have forgotten me. Invite him to sup with you, and say you wish to taste the wine of his country. He will go for some and while he is gone I will tell you what to do."

Aladdin and the magician.
Illustrated by Thomas Mackenzie

She listened carefully to Aladdin and when he left she arrayed herself gaily for the first time since she left China. She put on a girdle and head-dress of diamonds, and, seeing in a glass that she was more beautiful than ever, received the magician, saying, to his great amazement: "I have made up my mind that Aladdin is dead, and that all my tears will not bring him back to me, so I am resolved to mourn no more, and have therefore invited you to sup with me; but I am tired of the wines of China, and would fain taste those of Africa." The magician flew to his cellar, and the Princess put the

Illustrator: Louis Rhead

Illustrator: Charles Robinson

powder Aladdin had given her in her cup. When he returned she asked him to drink her health in the wine of Africa, handing him her cup in exchange for his, as a sign she was reconciled to him. Before drinking the magician made her a speech in praise of her beauty, but the Princess cut him short, saying: "Let us drink first, and you shall say what you will afterward." She set her cup to her lips and kept it there, while the magician drained his to the dregs and fell back lifeless.

Illustrator: Thomas Mackenzie (Above)

He fell backwards lifeless on the sofa.
Illustrated by Walter Paget (Right)

The magician drained his to the dregs and fell back lifeless.
Engraved by the Brothers Dalziel.

The Lady Bedr-el-Budur and the wicked magician.
Illustrated by Edmund Dulac

The magician drained his to the dregs and fell back lifeless.
Illustrated by Felix O. C. Darley

Illustrator: Casper Emerson

The Princess then opened the door to Aladdin, and flung her arms round his neck; but Aladdin put her away, bidding her leave him, as he had more to do. He then went to the dead magician, took the lamp out of his vest, and bade the genie carry the palace and all in it back to China. This was done, and the Princess in her chamber only felt two little shocks, and little thought she was at home again.

The Death of the African Magician.
Illustrated by H. J. Ford

The Sultan, who was sitting in his closet, mourning for his lost daughter, happened to look up, and rubbed his eyes, for there stood the palace as before! He hastened thither, and Aladdin received him in the hall of the four-and-twenty windows, with the Princess at his side. Aladdin told him what had happened, and showed him the dead body of the magician, that he might believe. A ten days' feast was proclaimed, and it seemed as if Aladdin might now live the rest of his life in peace; but it was not to be.

Illustrator: H. G. Theaker

The African magician had a younger brother, who was, if possible, more wicked and more cunning than himself. He traveled to China to avenge his brother's death, and went to visit a pious woman called Fatima, thinking she might be of use to him. He entered her cell and clapped a dagger to her breast, telling her to rise and do his bidding on pain of death. He changed clothes with her, colored his face like hers, put on her veil, and murdered her, that she might tell no tales.

Illustrator: Charles Robinson (Above)

On looking more attentively, he was convinced beyond the power of a doubt that it was his son-in-law's palace.
Illustrated by Milo Winter (Right)

For the villain had a brother yet more villainous than himself,
and a greater adept in necromancy.
Illustrated by René Bull

Illustrator: Walter Paget

Then he went toward the palace of Aladdin, and all the people, thinking he was the holy woman, gathered round him, kissing his hands and begging his blessing. When he got to the palace there was such a noise going on round him that the Princess bade her slave look out of the window and ask what was the matter. The slave said it was the holy woman, curing people by her touch of their ailments, whereupon the Princess, who had long desired to see Fatima, sent for her. On coming to the Princess the magician offered up a prayer for her health and prosperity. When he had done the Princess made him sit by her, and begged him to stay with her always. The false Fatima, who wished for nothing better, consented, but kept his veil down for fear of discovery. The Princess showed him the hall, and asked him what he thought of it. "It is truly beautiful," said the false Fatima. "In my mind it wants but one thing." "And what is that?" said the Princess. "If only a roc's egg," replied he, "were hung up from the middle of this dome, it would be the wonder of the world."

He changed clothes with her, colored his face like hers.
Engraved by the Brothers Dalziel.

Engraved by the Brothers Dalziel

After this the Princess could think of nothing but the roc's egg, and when Aladdin returned from hunting he found her in a very ill humor. He begged to know what was amiss, and she told him that all her pleasure in the hall was spoiled for the want of a roc's egg hanging from the dome. "If that is all," replied Aladdin, "you shall soon be happy." He left her and rubbed the lamp, and when the genie appeared commanded him to bring a roc's egg. The genie gave such a loud and terrible shriek that the hall shook. "Wretch!" he cried, "is it not enough that I have done everything for you, but you must command me to bring my master and hang him up in

**Illustrator:
Charles Robinson**

the midst of this dome? You and your wife and your palace deserve to be burnt to ashes, but that this request does not come from you, but from the brother of the African magician, whom you destroyed. He is now in your palace disguised as the holy woman—whom he murdered. He it was who put that wish into your wife's head. Take care of yourself, for he means to kill you." So saying, the genie disappeared.

When the Marid heard those words, his face waxed fierce and he shouted with a mighty loud voice.
Illustrated by René Bull

"My dear husband, what have you done?"
Illustrated by Walter Paget

Aladdin went back to the Princess, saying his head ached, and requesting that the holy Fatima should be fetched to lay her hands on it. But when the magician came near, Aladdin, seizing his dagger, pierced him to the heart. "What have you done?" cried the Princess. "You have killed the holy woman!" "Not so," replied Aladdin, "but a wicked magician," and told her of how she had been deceived.

After this Aladdin and his wife lived in peace. He succeeded the Sultan when he died, and reigned for many years, leaving behind him a long line of kings

Illustrator: Charles Robinson

Illustrator Biographies

Walter Crane

Walter Crane was born in Liverpool, England in 1845. The son of a successful artist, he obtained an apprenticeship at William Linton's engraving shop after his family moved to London. Impressed by his apprentice's work, Linton began to help Crane earn commissions, including one to provide the illustrations for J. R. Wise's book *The New Forest: Its History and its Scenery* (1862). During this time, Wise – a political and religious radical – introduced Crane to the work of John Stuart Mill and John Ruskin.

During the 1860s, Crane began to take an active role in politics as a supporter of the Liberal Party, and campaigned for the 1867 Reform Act. At the same time, his reputation as an illustrator continued to grow. Crane's first children's books, *The House that Jack Built* and *Dame Trot and Her Comical Gat,* were published in 1865. Over the course of his career, many more would follow, many of them known as 'toy books' due to their small length and size.

Throughout the seventies and eighties, Crane was a hugely prolific artist, producing a vast array of paintings, illustrations, ceramic tiles and other decorative arts. In 1888, he founded the Arts and Crafts Exhibition Society, and six years later worked with William Morris on one of his best-known works, *The Story of the Glittering Plain.* During the nineties, his easel pictures, such as 'The Bridge of Life' (1884) and 'The Mower' (1891), were exhibited regularly at the Grosvenor Gallery and elsewhere.

Crane died in 1915, aged 69. He is now regarded as the most prolific and influential children's book creator of his generation, and a major contributor to the development of the child's nursery motif in illustrated literature.

Illustrations on pages: xvi, 47, 61, 76.

The Dalziel Brothers

The Dalziel Brothers began as a duo – George Dalziel (1815-1902) and Edward Dalziel (1817-1905) – and were later joined by John Dalziel (c. 1820-c.1855) and Thomas Dalziel (1823-1906). The sons of artist Alexander Dalziel, they founded a highly successful engraving firm in 1839, through which they worked with many Victorian artists. Amongst other works, the Dalziel Brothers cut the illustrations to Edward Lear's *Book of Nonsense* and Lewis Carroll's *Alice in Wonderlnd* and *Through the Looking-Glass.* They also produced independent works, most notably *The Parables of Our Lord and Saviour Jesus Christ,* (1864). In their day, the Dalziel Brothers were the leaders in their trade, and examples of their work can be seen in the Victoria and Alberta Museum to this day.

Illustrations on pages: 4, 7, 22, 44, 48, 50, 54, 86, 90, 102, 112, 113.

Edmund Dulac

Edmund Dulac was born in Toulouse, France in 1882. He initially studied law at the University of Toulouse and the Académie Julian in Paris, before moving to London in 1904. Shortly after his arrival, the Frenchman won a commission to illustrate *Jane Eyre,* and under the ensuing relationship he developed with publishers Hodder & Stoughton, he illustrated editions of *Stories from The Arabian Nights* (1907), *The Tempest* (1908), *Stories from Hans Christian Andersen* (1911) *The Bells and Other Poems by Edgar Allan Poe* (1912), and many others.

Dulac became a naturalized British Citizen in 1912, and during World War I he contributed to a number of relief books, including his own *Edmund Dulac's Picture Book for the French Red Cross* (1915). After the war, his work spread into a number of other areas, including newspaper caricatures portraiture, theatre costume and set design, medals, and even postage stamps – including those issued to celebrate the coronation of King George VI (1937) and the 1948 Summer Olympics. Dulac died in 1953, aged 70.

Illustrations on pages: 23, 37, 43, 62, 71, 87, 95, 103

H. J. Ford

Henry Justice Ford was born in London, England in 1860. He was educated at Repton School and Clare College, Cambridge – where he gained a first class degree in the Classical Tripos – before returning to London to study at the Slade School of Fine Art. Starting in 1889, Ford began to produce the drawings for which he is now best-remembered, as part of *Andrew Lang's Fairy Books*.

In 1892, Ford began exhibiting paintings of historical and natural subjects at the Royal Academy of Art. Over the next two decades, while continuing to work on *Andrew Lang's Fairy Books*, he also illustrated *The Arabian Nights Entertainments* (1898) and *A School History of England by Charles Fletcher and Rudyard Kipling* (1911). Hailing from a family of enthusiastic cricketers, Ford also played a lot of high-level cricket, including with J.M. Barrie. He was also an acquaintance of P. G. Wodehouse and Sir Arthur Conan Doyle. Ford died in 1941, aged 81.

Illustrations on pages: 35, 60, 80, 106.

John Hassall

John Hassall was born in Walmer, Kent, England in 1868. He was educated at Newton Abbot College in Worthing, and Neuenheim College in Heidelberg, Germany. After graduating and twice failing to gain entry to The Royal Military Academy at Sandhurst, Hassall emigrated to Manitoba, Canada in 1888, where he joined his brother on his farm. During this time, he began to experiment with sketching.

Hassall returned to London two years later when he had some drawings accepted by the acclaimed periodical *Graphic*. At the suggestion of artistic friends, he studied art in Antwerp and Paris. During this time, he was heavily influenced by the famous poster artist Alphonse Mucha, and in 1895 he began work as an advertising artist for David Allen & Sons. He would remain here for fifty years, producing many well-known pieces, such as the 'Skegness is so Bracing' and 'Jolly Fisherman' posters (both 1908).

Hassall's style of flat colours and thick lines was well suited to children's books, and he produced many volumes of nursery rhymes and fairy stories. Amongst his best-known works was *Goose's Nursery Rhymes* (1909).

In 1901, Hassall was elected to the Royal Institute of Painters in Water Colours and the Royal Society of Miniature Painters. Between 1903 and 1904 he was president of the London Sketch Club, and opened his own New Art School and School of Poster Design in Kensington. Here, he counted Bert Thomas, Bruce Bairnsfather, H. M. Bateman and Harry Rountree among his students. Hassall died in 1948, aged 80.

Illustrations on pages: 3, 8, 19, 33, 69, 77, 82, 92, 119.

Thomas Mackenzie

Thomas Mackenzie was born in Bradford, England in 1887. He began producing illustrations for books shortly before the First World War, in a style highly reminiscent of his more famous contemporary Kay Nielsen. His earliest commissioned work was James Stephens's *The Crock of Gold,* which was published in 1913. Mackenzie followed this with *Ali Baba and Aladdin* and *Aladdin and His Wonderful Lamp in Rhyme* (both 1919), Christine Chaundler's *Arthur and His Knights* (1920) and James Elroy Flecker's *Hassan* (1924). During the twenties, Mackenzie moved to Paris, where he failed to make a career as a painter, despite spending time with Pablo Picasso. Mackenzie returned to England and passed away in 1944, aged 57.

Illustrations on pages: 13, 18, 21, 25, 27, 36, 46, 52, 57, 63, 67, 73, 74, 75, 81, 91, 97, 100.

Monro S. Orr

Monro Scott Orr was born in 1874, in Irvine, Scotland. The younger brother of artist Stewart Orr, he studied at the Glasgow School of Art, and went on to become one of Scotland's most popular book illustrators of the Golden Age. During his life, he exhibited at exhibited at the Royal Scottish Academy, the Royal Scottish Society of Painters in Watercolours, and the Glasgow Institute. Orr was fond of depicting figures, often without much background of context. Probably his most famous works are his version of *Arabian Nights,* and his watercolour map showing the history and distribution of the black death around the world.

Illustrations on pages: 29, 79.

Walter Paget

Walter Stanley Paget (1863-1935) was an English artist and illustrator whose fantastic work adorned books and magazines in late nineteenth-century and early twentieth-century London. Other notable works illustrated by Paget include: *"The Adventures of Sherlock Holmes"* (1891-93), *"The Hound of the Baskervilles"* (1902), and *"Thomas Hardy: A Bibliographical Study"* (1968).

Illustrations on pages: 11, 32, 93, 101, 111, 116.

Arthur Rackham

Arthur Rackham was born in London, England in 1867. One of twelve children, he first studied at the City of London School, where he won a number of prizes for his art. At the age of 18, Rackham became a clerk in the Westminster Fire Office, and continued to study part-time at the Lambeth School of Art. Around this time, he began to make occasional sales to the illustrated magazines of the day, such as *Scraps* and *Chums*. In 1891, he developed a close association with the *Pall Mall Budget* as one of the weekly's main illustrative reporters.

Beginning in 1892, Rackham left his clerk position at the Westminster Fire Office for the uncertainty of a career as an illustrator. He quickly secured a regular job as a reporter and illustrator at the *Westminster Budget*, a weekly magazine. At this stage, Rackham's illustrations were quite naturalistic in style, owing much to artists such as Howard Pyle. In 1893, his first book illustrations began to appear, and in 1896, his first whole book completed specifically on commissions was published, entitled *The Zankiwank and The Bletherwitch*. It featured the first hints of the fantastical, Gothic style for which he was to become known.

Rackham completed nineteen more book assignments during the 1890s, and continued to produce work at a good rate into the 20th century. In 1905, his first major, notable work appeared – a stunning version of the Washington Irving classic *Rip Van Winkle*, featuring 51 colour plates. A year later, another 50-plate work, *Peter Pan in Kensington Gardens*, appeared. In 1907, Rackham illustrated an edition of *Alice's Adventures in Wonderland*, and a redux of his earlier *The Ingoldsby Legends* appeared. By now, he was a well-known name, and his illustrations quickly became sought-after pieces of art.

Over the course of the rest of his life, Rackham illustrated a multitude of other works, including Shakespeare's *A Midsummer Night's Dream* (1908), Friedrich de la Motte Fouqué's *Undine* (1909), Richard Wagner's *The Rhinegold* and *The Valkyrie* (1910), *Aesop's Fables* (1912), J. M. Barrie's *Peter Pan in Kensington Gardens* (1912), Charles Dickens' *A Christmas Carol* (1915), *Cinderella* (1919), Shakespeare's *The Tempest* (1926), Edgar Allan Poe's *Tales of Mystery & Imagination* (1935) and – what is now considered his classic children's work, along with *Peter Pan in Kensington Gardens* – Kenneth Grahame's *The Wind in the Willows* (1940).

Rackham's works appeared in numerous exhibitions, including one at the Louvre in Paris in 1914. He died in 1939 at his home in Limpsfield, Surrey, England.

Illustrations on pages: 38, 83.

Louis Rhead

Louis John Rhead was born on 6th November 1857. He was an English-born American artist, illustrator, author and angler, who grew up in Etruria, Staffordshire, England.

Louis and all his siblings attended their father's art classes and worked in the potteries as children. His brothers Frederick Alfred Rhead and George Woolliscroft Rhead Jr. (1855-1920) were also artistic, and Louis, later in his career, sometimes collaborated with them – especially in his book illustration projects.

Because Louis demonstrated exceptional talent, when he was thirteen, his father sent him to study in Paris – with the artist Gustave Boulanger. After three years in Paris, Rhead returned to work in the potteries as a ceramic artist at Minton, and later at Wedgwood. After this considerable 'apprenticeship', in 1879, Rhead gained a scholarship at the National Art Training School in London. This was to be the start of his artistic career proper.

At the age of twenty-four, the young man emigrated to the United States. He had been offered a position as Art Director for the U.S. publishing firm of D. Appleton in New York City. Rhead accepted and moved to America in the autumn of 1883. The following year he married Catherine Bogart Yates, thus becoming an American citizen. Louis and Catherine lived in Flatbush overlooking Prospect Park for the next forty years.

In the early 1890s, Rhead became a prominent poster artist and was heavily influenced by the work of the Swiss artist, Eugène Grasset (1845 – 1917). During the poster craze of the early 1890s, Rhead's poster art appeared regularly in *Harper's* *Bazaar, Harper's Magazine, St. Nicolas, Century Magazine, Ladies Home Journal* and *Scribner's Magazine*. In 1895 he won a Gold Medal for 'Best American Poster Design' at the first International Poster Show in Boston.

By the late 1890s, the popularity of poster art declined and Rhead turned his skills to book illustration. Between 1902 and his death in 1926, Rhead illustrated numerous children's books published by Harpers and others. Most notable among these were editions of *Robin Hood, The Swiss Family Robinson, Robinson Crusoe, The Deerslayer, Treasure Island, Kidnapped* and *Arabian Nights*.

In his personal life, Rhead was an avid fly fisher, and by his own accounts started fishing trout between 1888 and 1890. Many of his later works deal with fishing and fly fishing – with his most famous and celebrated book being *American Trout-Stream Insects* (1916). At the time of its publication this was one of the first and most comprehensive studies of stream entomology ever published in America.

Louis Rhead died from a heart attack at his retirement home in Amityville, Long Island on 29th July, 1926.

Illustrations on pages: 5, 24, 45, 84, 98.

Charles Robinson

Charles Robinson was born in Islington, London, England in 1870. The son of an illustrator, and the brother of famous illustrators Thomas Heath Robinson and William Heath Robinson, he served a seven-year apprenticeship as a printer and took art lessons in the evenings. In 1892, Robinson won a place at the Royal Academy, but was unable to take it up due to lack of finances.

It wasn't until the age of 25 that Robinson began to sell his work professionally. His first full book was Robert Louis Stevenson's *A Child's Garden of Verses* (1895). The work was very well-received, going through a number of print runs. Over the rest of his life, Robinson illustrated many more fairy tales and children's books, including Eugene Field's *Lullaby Land* (1897), W. E. Cule's *Child Voices* (1899), Friedrich de la Motte Fouqué's *Sintram and His Companions* (1900), *Alice's Adventures in Wonderland* (1907), *Grimm's Fairy Tales* (1910) and Frances Hodgson Burnett's *The Secret Garden* (1911).

Robinson was also an active painter, especially in later life, and was elected to the Royal Institute of Painters in Water Colours in 1932. He died in 1937, aged 67.

Illustrations on pages: 14, 34, 59, 68, 82, 99, 108, 114, 117.

Harry G. Theaker

Harry George Theaker was born in Wolstanton, Staffordshire, England in 1873. His father was Headmaster of the nearby Burslem School of Art, where Theaker began his education, before moving on to the Royal College of Art. He quickly showed a great talent for painting, and after a period studying in Italy became one of the most widely respected watercolourists of the early 20th century.

Theaker exhibited widely during his lifetime, having several one man shows in London and elsewhere. Later in life, he became Head of the School of Art at the Regent Street Polytechnic, and a member of the Art Workers Guild. Aside from his landscapes, Theaker also produced decorative and stained glass, and provided illustrations for a number of books. Arguably his most famous children's book was *Stories of King Arthur,* published in 1925. Theaker died in 1954, aged 81.

Illustrations on pages: 17, 30, 55, 70, 78, 96, 107.

Milo Winter

Milo Winter was born in Princeton, Illinois, USA in 1888. He studied at Chicago's School of the Art Institute, and published his first illustrated book, *Billy Popgun* (1912), a year after graduating. Over the next few decades, he illustrated for Chicago publishers, such as Houghton Mifflin and Rand MacNally, as well as a number of East Coast publications. Arguably best-known for his animal drawings, Winter's best works were his editions of *Gulliver's Travels* (1912), *Tanglewood Tales* (1913), *Arabian Nights* (1914), *Alice in Wonderland* (1916) and *Aesop's Fables* (1919). Between 1947 and 1949, he was the art editor of Childcraft Books. Winter died in 1956, aged 68.

Illustrations on pages: 39, 109.

René Bull

Illustrations on pages: 9, 10, 31, 110, 115.

Felix O. C. Darley

Illustrations on pages: 2, 6, 15, 20, 28, 42, 85, 104.

Casper Emerson

Illustration on page: 150.

A. Guthrie

Illustration on page: 66.

Sidney H. Heath

Illustrations on pages: 12, 26, 40, 41, 51, 56, 58, 72, 94.

Robert Pimlott

Illustrations on pages: 16, 49, 64, 89.

Illustrations in this book has been sourced from the following titles:

Illustrator unknown. *Stories from the Arabian Nights' Entertainments.* **1859.**

A. Guthrie, Illustrator. *Aladdin and the Wonderful Lamp.* **1864.**

The Brothers Dalziel, Illustrators. *Arabian Nights' Entertainments.* **1865.**

Felix O. C. Darley, Illustrator. *Aladdin, or, The Wonderful Lamp.* **c.1873.**

Walter Crane, Illustrator. *Aladdin's Picture Book.* **1875.**

Sidney H. Heath, Illustrator. *Aladdin; or The Wonderful Lamp.* **1895.**

H. J. Ford, Illustrator. *The Arabian Nights Entertainments.* **1898.**

Walter Paget, Illustrator. *The Arabian Nights.* **1907.**

Robert Pimlott, Illustrator. *The Children's Treasure Book.* **1907.**

Casper Emerson, Illustrator. *The Arabian Nights.* **1910.**

Charles Robinson, Illustrator. *The Big Book of Fairy Tales.* **1911.**

René Bull, Illustrator. *The Arabian Nights.* **1912.**

Monro S. Orr, Illustrator. *The Arabian Nights.* **1913.**

Edmund Dulac, Illustrator. *Sinbad the Sailor and Other Stories from the Arabian Nights.* **1914.**

Milo Winter, Illustrator. *The Arabian Nights.* **1914.**

Louis Rhead, Illustrator. *The Arabian Nights' Entertainments.* **1916.**

Thomas Mackenzie, Illustrator. *Aladdin and His Wonderful Lamp In Rhyme.* **1919.**

John Hassall, Illustrator. *Aladdin.* **c.1920.**

H. G. Theaker, Illustrator. *Arabian Nights Stories.* **c.1924.**

Arthur Rackham, Illustrator. *The Arthur Rackham Fairy Book.* **1933.**

Printed in the USA
CPSIA information can be obtained
at www.ICGtesting.com
LVHW061234010224
770603LV00003B/46